Ghost Rescue

AND THE
GLOOMY GHOST TRAIN

Ghost Rescue

AND THE
GLOOMY GHOST TRAIN

WRITTEN BY
Andrew Murray

ILLUSTRATED BY
Sarah Horne

ORCHARD BOOKS

ORCHARD BOOKS
338 Euston Road, London NW1 3BH
Orchard Books Australia
Level 17/207 Kent Street, Sydney, NSW 2000
First published in hardback in Great Britain in 2009 by Orchard Books
First published in paperback in 2009
ISBN 978 1 84616 353 1 (hardback)
ISBN 978 1 84616 361 6 (paperback)
Text © Andrew Murray 2009
Illustrations © Sarah Horne 2009
The rights of Andrew Murray to be identified as the author and of
Sarah Horne to be identified as the illustrator of this work have been asserted by
them in accordance with the Copyright, Designs and Patents Act, 1988.
A CIP catalogue record for this book is available from the British Library.
1 3 5 7 9 10 8 6 4 2 (hardback)
1 3 5 7 9 10 8 6 4 2 (paperback)
Printed in Great Britain
Orchard Books is a division of Hachette Children's Books,
an Hachette UK company.
www.hachette.co.uk

In a graveyard in a town by the sea, three ghosts were being bullied. The other ghosts – rough, tough sailor ghosts – thought they were soft, silly and feeble.

"Does this scare you, Max?" sneered Land's End Larry. "OORRGAWWAAH!" he gurgled, pulling a face like a choking toad.

"Give us a kiss, Mary!" leered Salty
Sam. His horrible mouth gaped wide, as
if he were going to bite her head off.
"EEEEEAAAUUUUGGGHHH!"

"Who let rubbish like you into *our*
graveyard, Yatterdee?" snarled Harpoon
Harry. "GRRRUUUWWAAARRR!" he
howled, a sound that felt like icicles being
scraped against your brain.

One day, the fair came to that town by the sea, and Max, Mary and Yatterdee gazed longingly at it.

"What a wonderful place!" said Max.

"The big wheel!" said Mary. "The rollercoaster and dodgems! The candyfloss and coconut shies — and then there's the ghost train! What a time we would have, if only—"

"If only we could get away from the graveyard…" sighed Yatterdee.

But they couldn't. Their spirits were tied to the headstones of their graves. So there they stayed, prisoners of the graveyard, jeered at and sneered at by Land's End Larry, Salty Sam, Harpoon Harry and all the other sailor ghosts.

But then a man strode into the
graveyard. He was a grand man in a
top hat and golden waistcoat, a cheerful
man with a gleaming smile.

"I'm Boyman Briggs," he beamed, "the owner of the fair!"

Briggs had no fear of the sailor ghosts, and shooed them away.

Turning to Max, Mary and Yatterdee, he said, "How would you like to come with me to the fun and freedom of the fair? Escape the bullies forever? Have the good time you so richly deserve?"

The three ghosts jumped at the chance. Briggs chipped off a piece of each of their headstones and put them in his pocket, so that the ghosts could follow him, out of the graveyard – and into the fair.

Briggs led them past the ghost train
to his office. There was his grand desk,
there were his grand pictures around
the walls — and there was a safe, its
door open.

But then Briggs changed – his
gleaming smile turned into a sneer, his
bright face into a savage snarl.

"Fools!" he snapped. "Do you really think I care about a bunch of feeble ghosts? All I care about is my fair, and especially my ghost train ride – which is feeble indeed. The cardboard cut-out ghosts scare nobody these days, and the ghost train is losing me money.

What it needs is *scary* ghosts, and that's what *you* are going to do – be *scary*. And you had better be *really* scary – *or else*!"

Briggs took Max's stone and a metal file, and he began to grind the stone down, smaller and smaller.

"Owwww!" cried Max. "It hurts! Please, Mr Briggs, stop!"

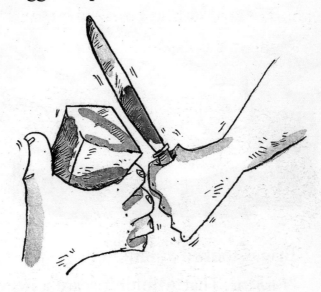

"You want me to stop?" said Briggs with a cruel smile. "Then SCARE ME!"

"W-w-what?"

"SCARE ME! NOW! Or I'll grind you into nothing!"

So poor Max tried for the first time in his death to be scary. He pulled a scary face, waved his arms and hooted, "Oooohhhhhhhh!"

Briggs looked at him in disgust.

"*Pathetic.* That wouldn't scare a nervous kitten. You'll have to do better than *that*." He held the file above Max's stone.

"N-n-no, please! Not the stone again!"

"Then SCARE ME, Max! I'm losing my patience!"

Max felt a sudden anger – what gave Briggs the *right* to do this to him? His face twisted into a horrible mask, he flew up into the air, and he shrieked in Briggs's face, "AAARRGGGHHUUGHYYYAHH!"

"Better!" smiled Briggs. "There's hope for you yet." He locked the three stones in the safe.

"Now, get along to the ghost train ride!" he snapped. "The next train starts soon — and I will be riding in it, to see how you do."

Max, Mary and Yatterdee hated Briggs. They hated him so much that they were *horribly* scary. The ghost train passengers screamed in terror — and they had a wonderful time! They all wanted another go, and another.

"Good," smiled Briggs. "But you had better keep it up – because if you ever stop being scary, *I will grind your stones down to dust, and you will cease to be…*"

That night, the ghosts sneaked into Briggs's office. They couldn't open the safe, so instead they used the computer to search for help. They typed in "ghost" and "rescue" – and found just the website they were hoping for…

Charlie and the Ghost Rescue team
(the ghosts of Lord and Lady Fairfax,
their daughter Florence, Zanzibar the dog
and Rio the parrot) were in Charlie's
room when the computer beeped to tell
them an email had arrived.

Dear Ghost Rescue,
Please help us! We are
trapped in a ghost train...

"How awful for those poor ghosts!"
said Charlie. "It's just like the way you
were all forced to perform by that
horrible Edwina Predder, up at Fairfax
Castle."

"Their seaside town," said Lady Fairfax,
"it's a long way off. We'll have to go in
the Ghostmobile."

So, with Zanzibar scampering ahead, and Rio fluttering above them, the team went out to the old pizza delivery van they used as a Ghostmobile.

As ever, Charlie was carrying a piece of the Fairfax stone in his bag so the ghosts could travel with him.

"Max, Mary and Yatterdee, here we come!"

Charlie climbed into the driver's seat,
and slid down to work the pedals and
hold the steering wheel. The ghosts acted
as his eyes and ears, telling him when to
start and stop and which way to turn.

The less said about the drive to the seaside and the fairground, the better. Lord F argued with Lady F and Florence about the best route. They took about a hundred wrong turnings, and nearly got stuck in a muddy field. They drove through three red lights, and almost ran over two squirrels and a frog.

They scraped the side of the Ghostmobile
against a wall, and stalled in the fast lane
of a motorway.

"Oh well," smiled Charlie. "Practice
makes perfect!"

And then they were there. Charlie
could smell the sea. There was the town,
there was the graveyard, and *there* was
Boyman Briggs's funfair.

Charlie bought a ticket for the ghost train, waited in the queue, and made sure to get a seat right at the back. *Clackety-clack!* The train set off. *Ba-dum-dum!* The doors bashed open. Into the darkness...

The passengers could see nothing,
until a shape loomed over them.

"OORRRRGAWWAAAHHHH!"
gurgled Max, pulling a face like a choking
toad. Everyone *screamed* – except Charlie.

"EEEEEAAAUUUUUGGGHHH!"
shrieked Mary, her mouth gaping wide, as
if she were going to bite their heads off.
Everyone *jumped* – except Charlie.

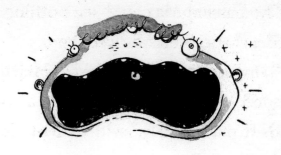

"GRRRRUUUWWAAAARRRRR!"
howled Yatterdee, a sound that felt like
icicles being scraped against your brain.

And everyone fearfully hugged their
neighbour – except Charlie. He just
unbuckled his seatbelt, quietly jumped off
the back of the train, and waited in the
darkness as the carriages rattled away.

"*You!*" cried Max.

"*Boy!*" shrieked Mary.

"*What are you doing there?*" howled Yatterdee. "*Aren't you AFRAID?*"

"Not particularly," said Charlie. "I'm from Ghost Rescue."

"Ghost Rescue? *You?* We were expecting a bit more than just one boy…"

"Come on out, guys!" smiled Charlie, and the Fairfax ghosts appeared.

There, in the darkness, interrupted by every ghost train ride, Charlie, the Fairfaxes and the ghost train ghosts talked.

"You've got to get the stones, Charlie," said Max. "Get the stones from Boyman Briggs's safe and then we can get away from here."

"You've got to open Briggs's safe," added Mary.

"But how am I going to do that?" Charlie asked.

"Wait till dark," said Yatterdee, "when Briggs and the fairground are asleep. We will all be your eyes and ears. Take Briggs's keys from his caravan, get into his office, and——"

"And how am I going to open the safe?" asked Charlie. "Do you know the combination number?"

"Er, no…" confessed Max. "But I can make myself small and go inside the lock. Then I can see what you need to do."

Charlie frowned. "Are you sure this will work? Because if it doesn't — and Briggs catches me — I don't want him to use me as a human cannonball…"

The moon shone silver on the velvet-blue world as Max, Mary, Yatterdee and Ghost Rescue surrounded Boyman Briggs's caravan. Rio perched on the roof and kept a lookout. Zanzibar sniffed for danger. And everyone else watched, and waited, and willed Charlie not to make a sound...

"Briggs is fast asleep," whispered Lord Fairfax. "*Go!*"

The key for the caravan was on the
other side of the lock. Charlie took
a sheet of newspaper and slid it
underneath the door. He stuck a pencil
in the lock and pushed the key out. It
landed with a faint *pat*.

Carefully, slowly, he pulled the
newspaper out from under the door —
and there was the key.

Charlie slid the key into the lock — holding it tight so it didn't rattle — and turned. The door opened. Charlie was inside the caravan.

He was breathing hard, and his heart was knocking at his ribs. He took a moment to calm himself.

Now – into Briggs's bedroom. It smelled eggy. Briggs must have just farted. There he was, his blanket rising and falling softly, steadily. And then came a *thrrrrp* sound – another fart.

On a chair were Briggs's trousers, with his key ring fixed to the belt. Charlie held the keys tight to stop them jingling – and fled, out of Briggs's room, out of the caravan. As he locked the door again, he breathed a sigh of relief.

But he didn't hold the key tightly
enough, and the lock rattled – *clackit-click*!

Did Briggs hear that? *Listen…* Briggs
was sleeping. All was silvery, velvety
quiet. Charlie had *done it*!

As he went to Briggs's office, Charlie's heart *boomed*, and his feet *thudded — boom-thud, thud-boom, boom-boom-thud!*

I'm the loudest person in the world! thought Charlie.

He unlocked the door to the office and stepped into the velvet-blue darkness.

He started to imagine Briggs waking up...seeing his keys missing...storming out of the door...

A door slammed. Charlie jumped.
"What was that?"

"It's OK," said Yatterdee. "It's just the
door to the ghost train, flapping in the
wind. Don't be afraid."

"I'm not afraid!" snapped Charlie,
afraid, and cross that he was afraid.

In Briggs's dream, the *clackit-click* of the caravan door as Charlie locked it became the *clickety-clack* of a ghost train. It was rushing along, with scary ghosts who smelled of farts, throwing him OUT at the end...

Briggs woke with a start. Something was wrong. There was a chill in the bedroom – and the door was open.

Funny, thought Briggs. *I'm sure I closed it.* He went to get his keys. Which were gone.

In Briggs's office, Charlie felt like a criminal. His heart pounded so hard that it felt bruised. His hands were clammy, and sweat stuck his shirt to his back. There, in the moonlight, was the safe.

"All clear," whispered Max. "I'm going into the lock now, and I'll tell you how to turn the dial. But because I'll be small, my voice will be too high for you to hear – so I'll speak in squeaks to Mary, and she can translate. Good luck, Charlie! *Good luuuck!*" he said in a voice that grew smaller and smaller, fading to a tiny mosquito buzz.

Charlie crouched down at the safe and put his sweaty hand to the dial. His heart went *boom-thud, thud-boom*, and suddenly it sounded like *footsteps*, creeping up behind him, right behind his back… *"Who's there?"*

"It's all right, Charlie," smiled Mary kindly. "There's nobody there, I promise. Zanzibar and Rio would tell us if there were!"

But, outside, Zanzibar was busy with a
rabbit burrow, and Rio had nodded off,
his beak drooping against his wing...

In his caravan, Briggs was turning the place upside down in search of the keys.

"No, no, no!" he cried, flying into a rage. "Stop to think for a minute. If someone took your keys, what would they do with them? Use them to turn on a ride, go on a rollercoaster in the moonlight?"

Briggs listened. The rides were all
silent.

"Use them to steal your car?"

Briggs looked. His car was still there
outside. The rides were safe, the car
was safe…

Safe.

"*The safe!*"

And Briggs *ran…*

Meanwhile, the sweat dripped from Charlie's hand. He heard the tiny mosquito buzz from inside the safe.

"Bzz-zzzz-zzzzzz-zzz-zz!"

"Left 21," whispered Mary.

"Bzzzz-zzzzzz-zzzz!"

"Right 17."

"Bzz-zzzz-zzzz-zz-zzz-zz!"

"Left 6."

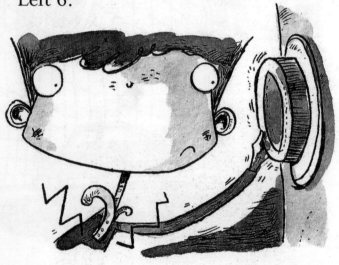

Oh, come on! thought Charlie. It was taking so long! *Boom-thud* went his heart…

Thud, thud, thud went Briggs's feet as he ran to his office.

"Steal from *me*, will they? Oh no, they don't know who they're dealing with!"

He slammed the door open. He switched on the light. And there, crouching in fear by the open safe, was a boy. He had the three ghost-stones in his hand, and was about to put them in his bag.

"Give them to me, boy," said Briggs.
Shaking with fright, Charlie handed
Briggs the ghost-stones. Briggs smiled.

"They put you up to it, did they?" he
said. "The ghosts? Max, Mary and
Whatshisname? They thought you could
fool *me*? The great Boyman Briggs?"

Briggs leant back and roared with laughter. Then he opened a cupboard, inside which was a toolbox. He opened the toolbox, inside which was a large hammer. And he put Max's stone on the floor.

"Max," said Briggs. "You'd better come here right now."

Max appeared.

"No, Briggs, please!" he pleaded. "Don't do it, don't do it please, we'll be good–"

"Too *late* to be good!" smiled Briggs.
He lifted the hammer, and SMASHED
the stone...

"*NO!* PLEASE, you're hurting me!"
cried Max.

Briggs POUNDED it...and pounded
Mary's stone...and Yatterdee's stone.

Max and Mary and Yatterdee screamed, and begged, and pleaded for him to *stop*, please *stop*... But they withered and shrank with every pounding of the hammer, until their stones crumbled to dust, and they faded away – gone, no more, dead ghosts... "*Noooooooooooooo...!*"

They were gone. Forever. Only Briggs and Charlie remained.

"Get out," said Briggs in a horribly
quiet voice. He dragged Charlie out of
the office, out of the fairground, and
threw him out of the gate.

"If I ever see you again, I'll take the
hammer to *you*!"

Charlie trudged into the night, his bag
sagging from his shoulder. Halfway
between the fair and the graveyard, he sat
down on a tree stump. His heart was
quiet now. There was only the moon,
and the wind.

He reached into his bag, and brought out the ghost-stones.

The real ghost-stones.

The ghost-stones he took from the safe — to be switched for three stones he had picked up from the ground. Three pebbles to put in the safe in their place. Charlie clenched them in his fist — and laughed!

And the Fairfaxes appeared – and laughed with him!

And Max appeared…

And Mary…

And Yatterdee…

And the moon and the wind were joined by one boy, and eight ghosts, laughing!

"Put our stones back in the graveyard,"
said Mary and Max.

"But are you going to be all right with
those graveyard bullies?" asked Charlie.
"Those hairy, scary sailor ghosts?"

Mary opened her mouth wide, and
shrieked. "EEEEEAAAUUUUGGGHHH!"

Max threw his head back, and *howled*.
"GRRRRUUUWWAAAARRRRR! We've
learned to be scary ourselves, Charlie!
We'll be all right. And Charlie?"

"Yes?"

"Thank you!"

"What about you, Yatterdee?" asked
Charlie.

"I've had enough of the graveyard," said
Yatterdee. "I want to help other ghosts.
I want to help Ghost Rescue. Will you
have me?"

"Is there room for one more in the Ghostmobile?" asked Charlie.

"With a squash," grinned Lord Fairfax.

"And a squeeze," chuckled Lady Fairfax.

"We'll all breathe in!" laughed Florence.

And the moon and the wind were
joined by a pizza delivery van – looking
very empty but which was actually very
full – driving off into the night.

Ghost Rescue

WRITTEN BY
Andrew Murray

ILLUSTRATED BY
Sarah Horne

Ghost Rescue	978 1 84616 358 6
Ghost Rescue and the Greedy Gorgonzolas	978 1 84616 359 3
Ghost Rescue and the Homesick Mummy	978 1 84616 360 9
Ghost Rescue and the Gloomy Ghost Train	978 1 84616 361 6
Ghost Rescue and the Horrible Hound	978 1 84616 362 3
Ghost Rescue and Mutterman's Zoo	978 1 84616 363 0
Ghost Rescue and the Dinosaurs	978 1 84616 364 7
Ghost Rescue and the Space Ghost	978 1 84616 366 1

All priced at £3.99

The Ghost Rescue books are available from all good bookshops,
or can be ordered direct from the publisher:
Orchard Books, PO BOX 29, Douglas IM99 1BQ
Credit card orders please telephone 01624 836000
or fax 01624 837033 or visit our website: www.orchardbooks.co.uk
or email: bookshop@enterprise.net for details.

To order please quote title, author and ISBN
and your full name and address.
Cheques and postal orders should be made payable to 'Bookpost plc'.
Postage and packing is FREE within the UK
(overseas customers should add £1.00 per book).

Prices and availability are subject to change.